Butter-Finger

Bob Cattell and John Agard

Illustrated by Pam Smy

F

FRANCES LINCOLN
CHILDREN'S BOOKS

Bowler man, bounce high,
Bowler man, keep low,
You meet your match in Riccardo.

Bowler man, bounce high,
Bowler man, keep low,
Riccardo ready with the willow.

Chapter 1

Willow trees didn't grow on his Island. There were coconut palms and tamarind, breadfruit and silk cotton trees. But no willow trees.

Riccardo had made lots of cricket bats: hacked them from the fronds of coconut palms, carved them from white driftwood, washed up on the beach. But he knew that the only true cricket bats came from the wood of the willow tree.

And now he had a proper bat of his own. It wasn't new. Bound up with tape to cover the splits and cracks in the blade, and with the string round the handle unravelling, it looked like a bat that had been pounded by ten thousand cricket balls. But it was his willow-tree cricket bat. Uncle Alvin had given it to him for his birthday, telling him, with a slap on the back and a toothy smile, that this was the bat that would launch the next great West Indian cricket star.

Riccardo was carrying it proudly over his shoulder as he arrived at *Calypso Cricket Club*.

Riccardo had played for *Calypso CC* just twice. To tell the truth, he wasn't a great cricketer yet. Though he practised as hard as anyone, he didn't seem to get much better. Being the team's 12th or even 13th man was the best he could really hope for and, when Natty had called him earlier that morning, he knew before he spoke that someone had dropped out.

"Richie and Mylo both sick," said Natty.

"Oh." Riccardo didn't want to sound too pleased.

"Would you believe it? Top of the League game against *The Saints*, man. Just when we need our best batting side, they get sick."

"So I playing?"

"Sure, man. I just tell you. Be there at 1.30, OK?"

Natty Tagore was *Calypso*'s captain. He was tall, athletic, a brilliant cricketer. His left-handed batting reminded Riccardo of Uncle Alvin's video of Garry Sobers playing at Lords. Natty had class: he'd already scored two centuries for the club this season and he could also bowl spin and swing. He was Riccardo's hero, but he wasn't always the most tactful of captains.

"What number am I batting?" Riccardo asked, regretting the question as he spoke.

"Dunno. Nine, maybe ten."

"Cool." But no way was it cool... Riccardo wanted to open the batting with Natty and score a century everyone would remember. He wanted to feel like Brian Lara after his 400-run world record. He wanted to be the best in the world.

o o o

He arrived at the ground far too early. The old pavilion was silent. There was no sign of any of the *Calypso* players or of the opposition. He wandered around looking at the fading photos of teams past and present which hung on the walls, all the time practising spectacular strokes with his new bat. An extravagant hook shot up-ended one of the silver cups on a trophy shelf above his head, and it came crashing down behind him.

"Who's that?" The shout came from the home changing room. He wasn't alone after all. Leo, *Calypso*'s opening fast bowler, appeared in the doorway. "Oh it's you, Small-boy. What you doing?"

Riccardo hated being called Small-boy. It wasn't a very smart nickname even for someone whose last name was 'Small' and who happened to be the shortest boy in his year at school. But he knew better than to show his feelings, especially to Leo. Leo was big and not very clever. He had big hands and big arms and big shoulders and on top of his big shoulders was his head. That is to say, his head grew straight out of his shoulders without anything resembling a neck. And it was a remarkably little head – not much larger than a fair-sized mango, with a sweet potato for a nose and completely shaved on top. The wrap-around shades were supposed to make him look mean and tough, but they perched on the only big things on his head: his ears. Leo's ears were like two banana leaves. They were like the handles of the silver cup that lay at Riccardo's feet. No wonder Riccardo's friend Bashy had nicknamed Leo Big Lug.

Riccardo bent down and picked up the cup, noticing with horror a big dent in its side. He replaced it carefully on the shelf. "I'm playing today," he said nonchalantly.

"No way! Who dropped out?"

"Mylo and Richie."

"Oh no. That's not funny. If we beat *The Saints*

today, we go top of the League."

"We'll beat 'em," said Riccardo stoutly, twiddling his new bat. But Leo shrugged and sucked his teeth and sighed as if to say, No chance. Not if you're playing.

The others began to turn up in twos and threes, throwing their bags carelessly on to the changing-room benches and greeting each other with noisy taunts. No one took much notice of Riccardo except for Bashkar Ali, the wicket-keeper. Like most of the *Calypso* players Bashy was a year older than Riccardo. Everyone said he was the best young keeper on the Island. Reactions like lightning, brilliant glove technique – nothing got past Bashy, especially when he was standing up to the spinners. Uncle Alvin said he had more raw talent than even Natty.

"New bat?" asked Bashy.

"Yeah. My uncle give me."

Bashy seized the bat and played a stylish cover drive. "Feels nice. It got a good middle?"

"Dunno," said Riccardo. "First time I play with it."

"You'll find out today – when we put on a big century together," said Bashy.

Riccardo grinned.

At that moment the band started to play. A cheer went up in the changing room. *Calypso CC* was the only team on the Island to have its own band. No one could remember whether the band or the cricket team came first, but everywhere the team went, Wesley and his Calypso Band went too. They played before the game, in the interval and, when things were getting really exciting, they even struck up between overs. They sang of famous *Calypso Club* victories and great West Indian triumphs around the world. They sang songs about centuries and hat tricks and catches. And there were a few rude songs, too, especially the ones about *The Saints* and *Windward Wanderers*.

Riccardo loved the band. The day after his first game for *Calypso*, he'd started composing songs for them to play and now he'd written hundreds. He wrote down his calypso lyrics in a little song book, which he kept with him at all times but never showed to a soul. One day he'd ask Wesley and the band to play his songs... when they were good enough.

The band's first song was always the *Calypso Club's* anthem, 'Bat and Ball'. Everyone knew the words and the changing-room echoed to the chorus as the whole team joined in with guitars, flutes, saxophones and steel drums blasting out the rhythm.

Today Bat and Ball will meet
In a sweet calypso beat.
I say today Bat and Ball will meet
In a sweet calypso beat.

Batsman beat the shine.
Bowler find your line.
When the band begin to play
Bat and Ball will break away.

Is Bat and Ball in motion,
Which one will be the champion?
Bat, show them your shots.
Ball, bounce on the spot.

No, the Saints don't stand a chance.
We'll show them the Bat and Ball dance.
Front foot, back foot, in-swing, out-swing,
Time for Bat and Ball to do their thing.

Chapter 2

Natty won the toss and elected to bat. Before opening the innings, he gave the batting line-up to the scorers. Riccardo was down at number 10. He'd have been 11 but for Leo, who was easily the worst batter on the Island. Leo held the club record for the most ducks in a season, probably because he always closed his eyes when the ball came towards him.

Natty and Desmond Drake opened the batting. Natty looked around the field and took guard. *The Saints'* fast bowler was already waiting at the end of his run-up, his eyes blazing. The band had stopped playing but their calypso was still ringing in the bowler's ears. The ground fell silent as he accelerated towards the crease and fired his first ball into the pitch. As it rose over his shoulder, Natty hooked. *Smack*! it went, off the middle of the bat and over the ropes for six. The little group of *Calypso* supporters rose to their feet and cheered... the game was on. And the band was soon in full swing again:

> Natty our captain,
> Natty our rock,
> Natty make the runs
> Run ahead of the clock.

50 came up in the first half-hour and *The Saints*' captain turned to his spinners.

"Watch out for this little guy," said Bashy, pointing to the new bowler. "He turn it both ways."

The Saints' spin bowler looked an unlikely cricketer. He was hardly taller than the stumps and for once Riccardo wasn't the smallest player in the game. The little spinner's first ball was swept savagely by Natty for four. So was the next, timed even more sweetly. The third ball of the over looked exactly the same to Riccardo. Natty thought so too and went for the sweep shot again. This time he missed completely and the ball thudded into his pad. The bowler's appeal for lbw was so loud it woke the parakeets in the palm trees. As they flew squawking across the pitch, the umpire raised his finger.

"That was the top spinner," said Bashy. "I told you this boy tricky."

'Tricky' was an understatement. The leg spinner took three more wickets in his next two overs, two clean bowled and one caught in the slips, and *Calypso* slumped to 68 for four wickets. There was a scurry of players rushing to the changing-room to put on their pads and plenty of advice about how to play the little magician who was bamboozling everyone.

Runs were now coming so slowly that Riccardo found himself cheering even the leg byes and the no-balls. The overs ticked by with the scoreboard hardly moving. Then an attempted quick single brought another disaster. A hesitation. A mix-up. And the ball came winging in to the bowler's end with both batters stranded in the middle. The only question for the umpires was, which one of them was out?

With 77 runs scored and five wickets down, Bashy walked out to the middle.

"Good luck," said Riccardo.

"Thanks. Don't forget our hundred partnership, man."

Bashy hit his first ball for two and then played a lovely drive for another couple of runs.

He appeared relaxed against the leg spinner, who was starting to look tired and even bowled a full toss which Bashy hit for four. As the hundred came up, the *Calypso* players and supporters cheered and clapped.

But Natty was getting anxious. "Not enough runs," he said, looking at the score book. "We need 150 minimum."

Leo boomed out the instructions to the batters with a voice like a foghorn: "C'mon, Bashy. C'mon, Ryan. Runs, man. Gimme runs." And Bashy responded with a pull for four. Unfortunately Ryan, who wasn't much of a batter, tried the same shot and skied the ball straight up in the air. The keeper made the steepling catch look easy.

The pressure mounted. And the new batter couldn't take it. With a head-in-the-air swipe he gave some easy catching practice to a grateful *Saints'* fielder. *Calypso*'s number nine lasted just two balls before he was given out lbw. And suddenly it was Riccardo's turn. He was looking for his batting gloves when Natty told him he was in. He found an un-matching pair, one red, one green, and pulled them on, grabbed his new bat and tumbled out of the changing room. On his way to the wicket he got his pads tangled up, stumbled and nearly fell over. The score stood at 111 for eight.

It was the end of the over, so Bashy was on strike. Five overs to go. "Plenty time," said Bashy, smiling confidently.

"Not for making a hundred partnership," said Riccardo.

"Fifty, then," said Bashy. "Push the single. I'll hit the boundaries."

"Easy to say push the single – I feeling so nervous I starting to tingle," said Riccardo. Bashy smiled at the rhyme and Riccardo felt a bit less shaky.

The opening bowler was brought back to finish his spell and Bashy sliced a quick ball in the air for four. Then Bashy was calling and Riccardo was running. He ran and ran. Two runs. Three more runs. And suddenly he was at the receiving end and it was his turn to face the fast bowler. The first ball was fired in at his toes, and he jammed his bat down on it just in time. He missed the next one and all the fielders groaned.

"Funny," said the wicket-keeper. "I swear that went through the stumps."

Riccardo concentrated grimly. He missed again,

got his bat tangled in his pads and nearly fell on the stumps.

"C'mon, Small-boy. You not playing a five-day test match," shouted Leo from the boundary. "Beat the ball."

"More chance with a fly swat than that old bat," said *The Saints'* keeper with a sly grin. Riccardo tried to ignore him.

At the end of the over, Bashy walked up to him again.

"Sorry," said Riccardo.

"Don't apologise, man. Put 'em under pressure. Tip and run."

Bashy showed the way and Riccardo followed – dropping the ball down in front of him and running hard. It was his first run and getting off the mark was a huge relief. Bashy opened his shoulders and drove a boundary straight over the bowler's head. Another single followed. Riccardo missed the next delivery, but it was called a wide. He then got a short lifter and instinctively stepped back and pulled. The moment the ball hit the bat he knew he didn't need to run. He felt the perfectness of it travel up his arms, through his body. The ball bounced once and flew across the rope. And he stood and watched it. And he thought,

I can do it. It should always be like this. He grinned at the keeper and patted his bat. Bashy met him in the middle and they slapped their gloves together triumphantly.

"Sweet four," said Bashy. "Three overs left. It's down to us. Don't expect any runs from Big Lug. He bats like a blindfolded donkey."

132 for eight. Back came the leg spinner for his final over. His first delivery turned past Bashy's bat and beat the keeper too. They ran a bye. Riccardo carefully marked out his guard again and watched the bowler run in. The ball fizzed in the air, pitched and spun. It was the googly. Riccardo, back on his stumps, flicked at it with the bat and missed. It clipped the top of his pad as it flew past.

"Howzat!" screamed the keeper, raising the ball high in his gloved hand.

"But I didn't touch it, man. It hit my leg."

A huge cheer went up. The umpire's finger was raised.

Riccardo stared down the pitch and saw Bashy shake his head.

He turned and walked slowly back to the pavilion. He'd been cheated out by the keeper and the umpire. He didn't say a word as he passed his team-mates on the bench by the pavilion and headed straight for the changing-room.

Leo edged a lucky single and Bashy fashioned another six runs off the spinner. The first ball of the next over sent Leo's middle stump cartwheeling out of the ground.

Calypso were 139 all out. Bashy had top scored on 42.

Chapter 3

Riccardo stood on the boundary, precisely where Natty had told him to field. Right out in the deep. He wished he were in the slips, chatting to Bashy about the fielding positions and the bowling. For the first five or six overs of *The Saints*' innings, the ball came nowhere near him and he tried to keep his concentration by walking in with the bowler and jogging up and down. But the more his legs moved, the more his mind wandered.

He imagined what Uncle Alvin would have said about his innings and that stupid umpire's mistake. Probably something like, 'Umpires are only human. Just forget about it and get on with the game.' Since his dad had left the Island to go and work in England, his uncle had been like a father to Riccardo. He'd taught him to love cricket and told him all about the great West Indian teams and of cricket legends like Malcolm Marshall and Vivian Richards and Michael Holding and Courtney Walsh and the greatest of them all, Garry Sobers.

Sobers was Uncle Alvin's all-time hero – 'Sir Garfield', as he called him. How many times had Riccardo heard the story of that July day in a place called Swansea, when the great left-hander had scored six sixes in an over? The first three balls had disappeared into the stands. The fourth was stroked over the scoreboard. The fifth was caught on the boundary but the fielder fell backwards over the rope and another six was signalled. And in his dreams, Riccardo would imagine the last ball soaring clean out of the ground into a green meadow lined with willow trees.

Uncle Alvin had a little poem about Sir Garfield and Riccardo knew it off by heart.

> Sir Garfield was his name
> and cricket was his game.
> A bat he loved to wield.
> A ball he loved to swing.
> See Sir Garfield
> on a cricket field.

and, man, you see a king.
He hit one six and he hit two six,
He hit three six and he hit four six,
He hit five six and he hit six six.
Six six in a row.
Licks-o licks-o!
Sir Garfield on de go.

"Oi! Small-boy. Wake up, man!" Riccardo saw Leo glaring at him, hands on hips. Suddenly there was the ball racing towards him, going to his left and travelling fast. He ran along the boundary to cut it off and, in desperation, thrust out a foot to stop it. Too late. It glanced off the toe of his trainer and bounced over the rope. Riccardo tripped on the rope and did a nose-dive into the hard ground.

Leo bellowed with anger and buried his head in his hands.

Natty walked slowly towards Riccardo, who picked up the ball and underarmed it to his captain without meeting his eyes. "Get your body behind it next time," said Natty. "We can't go giving away stupid boundaries like that."

Riccardo hung his head, rubbed his sore nose and walked back to his fielding position. He glanced at the scoreboard. *The Saints* had scored 34 without loss from eight-and-a-half overs. He watched Leo run in again and bowl. Maybe the fast bowler's frustration made him put a bit extra into the delivery, because it hit the pitch, took off with a puff of dust and caught the shoulder of the bat. Bashy was the first to react. He raced forward, dived, got a glove under the dropping ball and caught it. 34 for one. Bashy to the rescue, thought Riccardo thankfully.

From then on the balance of the match see-sawed, first one way then the other. *The Saints* advanced to 50 without further loss. Then two wickets fell in quick succession. But a partnership of 40 put the batting side on top again. Just 50 needed for victory now from 12 overs.

Natty brought himself on to bowl and immediately got the breakthrough with a sharp caught-and-bowled. A run-out followed soon after, thanks to a brilliant piece of fielding by Desmond Drake. The scoring rate dropped and slowly *Calypso* put the pressure on the new batters.

With six overs left and 33 runs needed, both batsmen self-destructed, skying catches to the deep. Leo came back and clean-bowled their little leg spinner, which made it 110 for eight.

The shadows were lengthening across

the ground and the band started up again with the old *Calypso* favourite,

> Today Bat and Ball will meet
> In a sweet calypso beat...

Twice the ball was knocked down to Riccardo and twice he raced in and fired back a low throw on the bounce, directly over the stumps. Bashy tapped his gloves together in appreciation.

Just as the target was looking to be beyond *The Saints*, their number 10 struck an enormous six. It was 130 for eight as the last over began – ten to win from six balls and two wickets in hand.

Natty threw the ball to Leo. The match swung back and forth with every ball. Two runs. One run. A wicket – clean bowled. One run. And then a four.

Leo shook his head angrily and walked slowly back to his mark for the final ball. *The Saints* needed two to win. Natty made the last adjustments to his field. The tall fast bowler started his run-up to the wicket. He leaned back, left elbow raised, the right arm came over and with a grunt he fired the ball down the pitch. The batter swung wildly. There was a sharp crack, a top edge.

The *Calypso* players looked up. Where was it? "Catch it, Riccardo! Catch it!" yelled Bashy.

Riccardo looked up. The ball was just a tiny dot in the dark blue sky. There was no doubt – it was coming his way. He took a couple of steps forward, then one to the side. Oh no, it was going over his head! He ran backwards, tripped, nearly fell and his hands went up to take the catch. Before he could steady himself he felt a sharp, hard crack at the base of his right thumb, left thumb bent back, a blow on the chest and the ball rebounded forwards. He lunged at it with one hand. Got the ends of his fingers to it. Juggled with it... but it looped away. And as he fell, he watched in anguish the ball bouncing across the hard earth.

Silence.

"Throw it!" screamed Bashy.

In panic, Riccardo scrambled to his feet and picked up the ball. If his throw had been on target it might have been a run-out, but Bashy had to scurry to his left to retrieve it. And *The Saints* pair were through for the second run. A big cheer from behind him told Riccardo the terrible truth: *The Saints* had won. He had handed them victory at the last gasp.

The two batters jogged past him with broad grins on their faces, bats raised high. And then the *Calypso* team straggled in. No one said a word to him. Leo glared. A couple of the others shook their heads grimly. Finally, Bashy walked up to him and patted him on the shoulder. "Hard luck. You did your best."

Riccardo felt the tears stinging at the back of his eyes and turned away. And then the band began to play very slowly:

> Butter-Finger
> catching a ball,
> Butter-Finger
> must make it fall,
> Butter-Finger
> fetching a plate,
> Butter-Finger
> must make it break.

Chapter 4

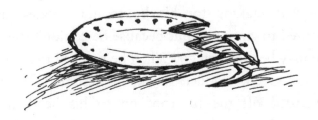

Riccardo didn't waste time. He grabbed his T-shirt and jeans from the changing room and ran. He didn't stop until the sound of the band had faded and by then he was more than halfway up the hill to his village. When he stopped, the blood pounded in his head with an all-too-familiar rhythm.

> Butter-Finger
> catching a ball,
> Butter-Finger
> must make it fall.

It began to rain, splattering through the leaves of the trees and exploding in bucketfuls across the track. As he reached the village Riccardo recognised the familiar shapes of his neighbours rushing to take cover from the downpour.

He walked steadily on, straight through all the puddles, scarcely aware of where he was going. He was making for his house not because he wanted to go home, but because he couldn't think of anywhere else to go. When he reached the door of the green, wooden shack, he hesitated. Water cascaded off the tin roof on to his head and plastered his cricket shirt against his back. Inside the house, he could hear his mother and big sister, Martha, talking. He opened the door and went in.

Jessie was first off the mark to greet Riccardo. She was *his* dog. They'd grown up together. But Jessie wasn't really interested in him. Food was always the first thing on her mind. After nosing his pockets greedily, she returned to her prime pouncing position under the kitchen table, where there was an excellent chance of a piece of *roti* falling her way.

"Look at you, you're soaking. And I've just washed this floor," said Riccardo's mother. "Go get out of those wet clothes right away."

"What wrong with your nose? It's squashed," said his sister.

"I done it fielding," Riccardo mumbled.

"I thought rain wash out the game," said his sister.

Riccardo shook his head.

"You got beat, then. I can tell from your face." She laughed.

"Dinner in half an hour," said his mother, wiping the roti flour off her hands. "Why you don't get those wet clothes off and go talk cricket with Alvin?"

Uncle Alvin lived just two doors away but he was the last person Riccardo wanted to see. He'd be sure to ask him how many runs he'd scored with his new bat. And what would Uncle Alvin say when he told him about the dropped catch? Riccardo went to his room, put on some dry clothes and slipped out again.

● ● ●

The rain had stopped. Fireflies were flickering around the dripping trees, daubs of yellow, darting, dancing, dying. Riccardo sat on an old wooden trailer that belonged to the chicken man who lived in the yellow house, and pulled his song book out from under his T-shirt. The little book wasn't anything special. It was smaller and thicker than his school exercise books. Just an ordinary notebook, except that it was bright red and there was something about the way it felt that he really liked.

He wrote down from memory all the words of the Butter-Finger calypso. Then, on the facing page, he wrote a song of his own:

They making fun of me in calypso
Calling me Butter-Finger and it hurt so.
They won't let me forget the catch I drop.
Teasing me till I feel like a flop.

But one day, one day I'll be a hero.
My time will come, 'King of the Willow'.
Butter-Finger will have the last laugh
When they line up for my autograph.
Yes, when I'm in the hall of cricket fame
They will glad to know Butter-Finger name.

I had no excuse, I couldn't lie,
Couldn't say the sun was in my eye.
One minute the ball in my hand,
Next minute the ball on the ground.
I let the team down, I let myself down.
I learnt the meaning of humiliation.

But one day, one day I'll be a hero.
My time will come, 'King of the Willow'.
Butter-Finger will have the last laugh
When they line up for my autograph.
Yes, when I'm in the hall of cricket fame
They will glad to know Butter-Finger name.

He had just written the last word when a familiar voice behind called out his name. "Hey, Riccardo. I brought your bat back." It was Bashy. Riccardo pushed the red book under his shirt. He'd forgotten about the bat, left behind in the changing room.

Bashy sat down beside him on the trailer. "Everyone's dropped one of those," he said. "They always tricky. And it was nearly dark."

"But the sun was out."

"Too bright, then," said Bashy helpfully.

Riccardo shrugged. "Make no difference. We lost... and everyone think is my fault."

"No they don't. That's stupid."

"What about Leo, then?"

"Big Lug? What's the matter with you? Who cares what he thinks?"

In spite of himself, Riccardo nearly smiled. Bashy kept up the offensive. "I can't understand

34

how he could bowl with ears like that. One of these days he take off before he reach the crease."

"What about that song, then?" said Riccardo.

"What song?"

"The Butter-Finger one."

"Take no notice. You know what Wesley and the band like."

"It wasn't funny."

"That's calypso, man," insisted Bashy. "You make up the words. Sometimes they funny. Sometimes they cruel. Everyone soon forget."

"Well, I won't forget."

"You coming to the beach tomorrow?" asked Bashy, changing the subject fast.

"Maybe," said Riccardo. He and Bashy hardly ever missed Sunday morning's beach cricket game. But he wasn't likely to be going tomorrow. He got up from the trailer. "Thanks for the bat. Gotta go now." He left his friend sitting there and went home.

● ● ●

Dinner was Riccardo's favourite – goat curry and roti bread – but he hardly noticed the food.

"Little Ricci got the blues," said Martha,

in a stage whisper.

"Please leave him alone, Martha," said their mother.

Martha never knew when to stop. "Who dropped a catch and lost the match?" she taunted.

"That's enough, Martha."

"Who told you?" demanded Riccardo crossly, as his mother went to get the pudding.

"Who told me? The whole island knows."

"What you know about cricket?" Riccardo said defiantly. Jessie's nose poked up from under the table in search of food and Riccardo pushed her away angrily.

"I know if you drop the ball, it's not out," laughed Martha. "Hey, catch." She lobbed a spoon towards Riccardo and it bounced off his arm and clattered to the floor. Jessie pounced on it optimistically. "Oh sorry, I forgot you can't. Can't catch 'cos he's so clumsy!"

Riccardo picked up another spoon to throw at Martha and knocked his ginger beer flying.

"Idiot!" screamed Martha, "Look what you done, you clumsy fool. You ruined my new jeans." She jumped up, knocking over a plateful of rotis, and the china shattered on the hard floor. Jessie was on them in seconds and quickly withdrew into a corner of the room with a roti as a prize.

"What going on here?" demanded his mother, storming back into the room. "Clear that mess up immediately, Riccardo."

"But I didn't ..."

"You heard me."

Riccardo stood up, knocked over his chair and ran out of the room, slamming the door behind him so hard that the door-frame rattled.

Chapter 5

There are always big crowds at the beach for the cricket game on Sunday mornings. And anyone can play. Sometimes there are 25, 30 or more players a side, with even guest appearances from some of the Island's first-team stars. But one thing never changes: every Sunday the same two teams compete – *Neptune* against *Pirates* – and if you play cricket on the Island, you are either a *Neptune* or a *Pirate*.

Riccardo and Bashy were Pirates. It was on the Caribbean sands, with a bouncy taped tennis ball, that they'd learned to play. Younger kids had taken their regular places in the *Pirate* team now, but Riccardo and Bashy still came along most Sundays just to have a bat or a bowl or field for half an hour.

The game was in full swing when the two friends arrived. *Neptune* were batting. They were 96 for five wickets or 95 for six, depending on who you talked to. The umpires were supposed to keep count but it was a tradition for the crowd to argue about the score.

Bashy, always a popular figure with the beach *Pirates*, was immediately dragged out to the middle and given the keeper's gloves. He quickly repaid their faith with a lightning stumping down the leg side.

Riccardo stood under a coconut tree watching. He didn't feel like playing today. If it hadn't been for Bashy he wouldn't have come. He noticed Leo over by the roti stall with three of his big-mouth *Neptune* mates, Snapper, K-man and Brian. You could hardly miss them. They were singing songs with weird words and making fun of the *Pirate* players. Some people are so stupid, they don't even know they're stupid, thought Riccardo.

He waited alone till Bashy returned. Then Uncle Alvin appeared, too. Uncle Alvin never missed a *Neptunes* v. *Pirates* game. "Smart glove work," he said to Bashy. "Reminds me of when I kept wicket

here to the great Lance Gibbs. I was about your age." The sentence trailed off with Uncle Alvin's trademark laugh – somewhere between a wheeze and a chuckle – and, when he laughed, his mouth seemed at least two sizes too big for his face. He launched into one of his favourite old calypsos, improvising the words as he sang:

Cricket, lovely cricket
On a beach where I played it
With those little pals of mine
Under the tropical sunshine.
The palm trees waving at me
And all the sea for my boundary.

Cricket, lovely cricket
On a beach where I played it.
Here is where many Greats begin
To learn the art of bounce and spin,
And every time you hook a four,
Hear the seagulls cheering for more.

Cricket, lovely cricket
On a beach where I played it.
Brown sand was our village green,
The trade winds spectating the scene,
I bet even Lord's Cricket Ground
Don't have palm trees all around.

"Lance Gibbs was too old to play for the West Indies by then," continued Uncle Alvin. "but he could still turn a ball half a metre and make it bounce high as your head. He told me I was a good young keeper, but I was never nearly as good as young Bashkar here."

Bashy laughed. It was far from the first time he'd heard the Lance Gibbs story but he liked Riccardo's uncle's yarns. "I'd love to keep wicket to a world-class spin bowler," he said.

"You'll be playing for the West Indies in ten years – I'll bet my rum shack on it," said Uncle Alvin.

He began another calypso, waving to his friends in the crowd and swaying his shoulders to the rhythm.

Riccardo felt a twinge of jealousy, even though he knew that Bashy deserved every bit of his uncle's praise. Bashy was a great keeper and a fine batter and he, Riccardo, couldn't even catch a cricket ball. He didn't want to give Uncle Alvin a chance to talk about yesterday's game and, driven by a sort of panic, he walked away from his uncle and Bashy and out to field for the *Pirates*. The *Neptune* batter had just belted a six off a young spinner – slogged it straight into the sea. The *Neptune* supporters were howling with delight.

"Hit him over the trees, Calvin!" shouted Leo. "Hit the donkey off the Island." Suddenly Big Lug spotted Riccardo. "Hit it over here, Calvin. Slog it in the air to Butter-Finger. He can't catch a cold."

There was a cackle of laughter from Leo's stupid friends and then a hush as the bowler ran in. Calvin's big bat swung and launched the ball high in the air. Higher and higher it went and, as it started its descent towards Riccardo, the cries turned to a mocking *ooooOOOOOH*. Everyone knew what was going to happen next. His whole body shaking, Riccardo watched the ball getting bigger and bigger. It bounced into his hands … and bounced straight out again.

But that wasn't the end of it. Another fielder had been running towards the ball. She ran fast with her eyes fixed on her target and she didn't see Riccardo until the very last minute. As the ball bounced out of his hands she collided with him…

and little Riccardo went flying across the sand. Lying there on his back, he saw the ball loop upin the air and, as if in slow motion, land straight in the girl's hands. She threw it high in triumph and then she looked down at Riccardo, and giggled.

Leo led the hoots of laughter that rang around the beach. It seemed as if the whole world was laughing, laughing and jeering at Riccardo.

He turned for help to Uncle Alvin and Bashy. But they were laughing, too. He couldn't believe his eyes: tears of laughter were running down Uncle Alvin's cheeks. Some of the younger *Pirates* ran over to congratulate the catcher and they gathered round Riccardo chanting in high-pitched voices, "*Butter-Finger, Butter-Finger, Butter-Finger, Butter-Finger*". Riccardo's legs went weak. He wanted to vanish like a magic genie back into the bottle. He had to escape. The laughter continued and he swung wildly at the grinning faces again and again. But they wouldn't move and his blows fell on thin air.

⊙ ⊙ ⊙

And then he woke up.

He was hammering at the pillow with his fists. The laughter had died away. It had all been a horrible dream.

Chapter 6

The days went by. Riccardo spent more and more time on his own, restlessly stalking the tracks and paths of the Island. Sometimes, when he couldn't be bothered with school, he'd wander miles inland or along Constantine beach to the Smuggler's Rock. Jessie often joined him at the start of his journeys, but some irresistible and disgusting thing to eat in a dustbin or a rubbish heap soon distracted her from venturing further.

Riccardo liked being alone, watching the bumboats across the bay, going out in the mornings for king fish and flying fish, or listening to the women singing and laughing in the cocoa fields. Every day he wrote at least one new song in his red book. These weren't cricket calypsos but strange chants and poems about himself and his Island. He called them his Angry Songs, and when he was alone in his room at night he rapped out the rhythms.

Martha said he was becoming weird and it wouldn't be too long before he was sleeping in a cave full of bats and living like a hermit on raw plantains and breadfruit. "They'll call you Barmyboy or Caveman," she said. *Makes a change from Butter-Finger*, thought Riccardo.

◎ ◎ ◎

One day, sitting alone under a coconut tree, look-ing miles along the coast towards the Calypso cricket ground and his vil-lage beyond, he wrote this little song. It became his favourite chant and he'd often sing out the words or whistle the tune as he walked along.

> **Coconut tree,**
> **I feel your majesty,**
> **Do you feel my misery?**

46

Coconut tree,
Bet you've never been teased
For having butter-finger leaves.

Coconut tree,
You have every right to be proud,
But I'm the one facing the crowd.

Coconut tree,
Under your shade I'll stay
Till this pain goes away.

The only *Calypso* players he saw were Bashy and Leo. Bashy often came to see Riccardo in the evening and, as he chattered away, he didn't seem to notice that his friend hardly spoke a word.

Leo was the only member of the team who went to the same school as Riccardo, which was one of the reasons why he skanked off so often. Riccardo always felt that Big Lug was sneering and laughing behind his back and he spoke to him only when he'd got something to boast about.

"Five for 27 on Saturday, Small-boy," Leo would say with a toothy grin that made his ears look like the twisted ends of a sweet wrapper.

"Oh good. Did you win?"

"Win? We murdered them. Five wickets! And that Natty took me off! I guess he had to give the other bowlers a chance. They score 120. We knock them off for two wickets."

"Did you bat?"

Leo glared at Riccardo. "Course not, stupid. I'm a fast bowler. You know nothing about cricket, Butter-Finger."

Riccardo shrugged and walked away. He already knew about the victory, because Bashy gave him a ball-by-ball commentary of every *Calypso* game. After their defeat by *The Saints*, they'd now won three in a row and, although they were still second in the league to *Wanderers*, they'd progressed to the quarter finals of the Island Cup.

"You want to play, Saturday?" said Bashy one day.

"Don't be stupid. You know Natty never going to pick me again."

"Seriously, man. We've got so many injuries and..."

"I ain't playing. I'm not playing cricket no more... especially not for *Calypso Cricket Club*," said Riccardo, with a snarl of anger that took him by surprise.

"OK," said Bashy. "Do what you want. None

of my business."

Natty didn't ring. And a couple of days later Riccardo made the fateful decision. He was never going to play cricket again as long as he lived – and so he didn't need a stupid cricket bat. He took his uncle's precious present from under his bed, walked down to the beach and gave the bat to a young Pirate player called Kinsale. Kinsale was delighted.

Riccardo didn't tell anyone about the bat, but of course, it wasn't long before Martha the Mouth heard the news, and the first person she told was Uncle Alvin. Riccardo expected him to be angry, but he wasn't. Or if he was, he didn't rant and rave. Uncle Alvin said something about quitting at the first hurdle and after that he never mentioned the bat again. He stopped talking to Riccardo about cricket, too. Not another word about Sir Garfield or Lara's 400 world record or any of the great West Indies heroes.

⊙ ⊙ ⊙

One day, when Riccardo was walking alone in an unfamiliar part of the Island, he heard a band playing. As he got closer, he realised it wasn't just any band. It was *Calypso CC*. They were playing away against *Santa Maria CC* and Wesley and his musicians were pounding out the music. For the rest of the afternoon he watched the match from a distance. Watched and listened to the beat of the calypsos echoing around the hills. As Riccardo took in the words and the rhythms, he wrote furiously in his little red book, copying down four of Wesley's latest calypsos and writing three Angry Songs of his own. His favourite was the one which had Leo getting hit for six sixes in an over.

Calypso won easily. Bashy scored a lightning-quick 75 and the *Santa Maria* batting collapsed. Worst of all, Leo took another five wickets.

As Riccardo walked home in the twilight, he was overtaken by a happy, whistling Bashy.

"Hey, Riccardo, what you doing here?" asked Bashy. When Riccardo didn't reply, he added, "We beat *Santa Maria* in the quarter final of the Island Cup."

"I saw it. You batted like a boss."

"Where you hiding?"

Again Riccardo didn't answer.

"First time we make the Cup semi finals," said Bashy, refusing to allow his enthusiasm to be dampened by his friend's silence.

"Who you playing?"

"*Waterloo*. They knock us out last year. You coming to watch?"

"No, thanks."

"What you got there?" Bashy pointed to the book that Riccardo held in his right hand.

"None of your business."

Bashy looked hurt. Then he strode off ahead of Riccardo. He was ten metres away when he turned and said, "I don't care what you think of Natty and Leo and the team. I don't care if you like cricket or hate cricket. But I'm your friend and you don't ever speak to friends like that." He broke into a run, and after a bend in the track Riccardo saw no more of him.

At that moment Riccardo realised things were getting out of hand.

Chapter 7

The next day Riccardo skanked off school again. Jessie followed him along Harbour Road to the Oval, the Island's main cricket ground. None of the dustbins on the way showed much promise, so she was still within sniffing distance of Riccardo as he walked through the main gates and sat down on a bench next to the pavilion. There was no game on and the ground was empty... or almost. A single figure could be seen out on the pitch and Riccardo recognised him immediately. Count Crawfish was the most famous person on the Island. Everyone knew the words of *That ain't cricket, man, Cricket philosophy*

and his other bestselling songs. Count Crawfish, three-times winner of the Calypso Championship, was so famous that no-one could quite understand why he'd taken the job of groundsman at the Oval – though Uncle Alvin said he was the best groundsman in living memory.

Count Crawfish was mowing the outfield, seated on an ancient, ear-splitting motor lawn-mower, and Riccardo took out his little red book and started to write a song to the rhythm of the spluttering machine. Suddenly the engine stopped, there was a loud shout and Riccardo looked up and saw the Oval groundsman leap from his mower, with amazing agility for an old man, and dash in the direction of the pavilion.

"That damn dog!" he shouted. "Stop him! He's got my dinner."

Riccardo just caught sight of Jessie disappearing round the corner of the pavilion at a steady lope. In her jaw was a large grey bundle. *Time to get out of here*, he thought. He leapt over the back of the seat and was safely out of the ground in seconds. As he stopped to catch his breath and look around for his thieving dog, he realised with a lurch in the pit of his stomach that something was missing, something important. His little red book with all his precious calypsos and songs was still lying on the bench in the Oval ground.

His first and only thought was that he had to get it back. He ghosted into the ground, keeping to the shadow of the pavilion. But, as the bench came into view, he saw something which brought back his worst fears. There sat the old groundsman. And he was reading Riccardo's book.

Riccardo must have made a slight noise as he stepped forward into the sunlight because Count Crawfish suddenly glanced over his shoulder.

"Is this yours?" he asked in a quiet but authoritative voice.

Riccardo nodded.

"And that damn dog? Yours, too?"

Another nod.

"Well, it's eating my dinner. So you can read me your poems. Come here."

"I'm sorry," mumbled Riccardo. "She's very greedy."

"What's she called?"

"Jessie."

"So while Jessie enjoys my patties and samosas you'll entertain me. Agreed?"

Riccardo sat down on the bench beside Count Crawfish. He knew there was nothing to fear from this strange-looking old man. He had a wispy grey beard, a large, hawk-like nose and the kindest grey eyes which twinkled as he spoke. He calmly handed the book back to Riccardo, who read his favourite Angry Song.

"Now sing it to me," said Count Crawfish. And Riccardo sang.

"Hmm. And you wrote all these?"

"Yes. ... well, most of them."

"They not bad. So what's your name?"

"Riccardo Small."

"Small? Any relation of Alvin Small?"

"He's my uncle."

"He never tell me he has a Calypso Boy for a nephew. Sing me another song."

This time Riccardo chose *One day I'll be a hero* and the Count smiled broadly behind his beard as he listened. His grey eyes twinkled with pleasure.

"When Riccardo had finished, the Count said, "Now hear this. It's a little song about a hungry groundsman and a greedy dog." He bowed theatrically to Riccardo, who blushed as he remembered what Jessie had done. This is what the Count sang:

Somebody tell me what's going on,
I turn me back and me roti gone.
I've seen many wonders under the sun
But I never yet see a roti run.

Soon my roti was making the news
And sly Mongoose getting accused.
Remember how he went in a kitchen
And thief way a lady big fat chicken?
Mongoose real name is Rikki-Tikki-Tavi,
Who Mongoose fooling with false identity?
Rikki-Tikki-Tavi that Mongoose tricky,
Everywhere the talk is Mongoose guilty.

Now look at Count Crawfish predicament,
I don't like to blame the innocent,
How you can point a finger at Mongoose
When you see a hungry Dog on the loose?

I turn me back and me roti gone,
Free Rikki-Tikki-Tavi, he ain't the one,
I turn me back and me roti gone,
Free Rikki-Tikki-Tavi, let justice be done.
I don't care if Dog is Man's best friend,
I mean to clear Mongoose name in the end.
One day I'll sell my story to the press
And make sure that Doggie get arrest.

As the song came to an end, Riccardo was smiling. From behind them came a mighty belch. Jessie sat there, licking her lips loudly with a look of complete innocence. Count Crawfish's head rocked back and he roared with laughter. And Riccardo found that he was laughing too... laughing for the first time in weeks. The old groundsman put an arm around his shoulder and they both laughed till it hurt.

● ● ●

From that day, Riccardo went to see Count Crawfish three or four times a week. Jessie always came too, and usually got at least one roti or patty for her trouble. The old calypso singer never asked Riccardo why he wasn't at school. With his head tilted to one side, he would listen to the young boy singing his latest songs and poems. Sometimes he'd join in, repeating the chorus. And sometimes he'd stop Riccardo in the middle to suggest another word or say something about the story. But he always applauded long and loud at the end of each performance.

Each time Riccardo sang a song, Count Crawfish would respond with one of his own.

He sang old calypsos and brand new ones, showing his young pupil all the tricks of his trade. Riccardo was quick to learn. He listened to the new rhythms and remembered the funny rhymes he heard. He began by copying whole lines from the Count's songs into his own calypsos and poems. But then he found new words and rhymes of his own.

One day Count Crawfish said to him, "Why do you write songs, Rikki-Tikki-Tavi?" Riccardo had never liked his name being shortened to Ricky or Ricci, but Rikki-Tikki-Tavi had a nice ring to it.

"Dunno why I write them," he said.

"Nobody forcing you?"

"Course not."

"You writing them for someone else?"

"No."

"You think they'll make you famous?"

"No."

"Then why?"

"No reason. They just come into my head and I write them down."

"Then you a true poet, Rikki-Tikki-Tavi."

Chapter 8

The old tale of Rikki-Tikki-Tavi was one of the many that Riccardo heard for the first time from Count Crawfish. Rikki-Tikki was a mongoose. Riccardo knew all about mongooses: how, though no bigger than cats, they are formidable snake-hunters. Rikki-Tikki-Tavi was no exception.

The story of Rikki-Tikki-Tavi's adventures begin in a great flood. He is saved from drowning by a boy called Teddy. In return he saves Teddy's life and takes vengeance on the great black cobras, Nag and Nagina.

Young Rikki-Tikki-Tavi learns his skills in battle. Like all mongooses, he faces up to his enemy, dancing with a peculiar rocking, swaying motion that lets him attack from any angle and jump away from the snake's deadly strike. His victory over Nag brings down the dreadful vengeance of Nagina upon him. Rikki-Tikki is dragged into her black snake-hole. But after a terrible fight, the little mongoose emerges once again as the conqueror. Nagina is dead and all the birds sing of Rikki-Tikki, with eyeballs of red, who has delivered them from the deadly cobras.

The story of the little mongoose and the big snakes made Riccardo's heart leap. It was a story he'd never forget as long as he lived and later he made up many songs of his own about little Rikki-Tikki, the all-conquering hero. As he walked home that day with Jessie he chanted happily to himself, Rikki, the valiant, the true, Tikki, with eyeballs of flame.

◦ ◦ ◦

"Talk to me about cricket," said Count Crawfish one day.

"I don't like cricket no more," said Riccardo, avoiding the Count's eyes.

"Oh, is that so? You like to hear a cricket calypso?"

"No."

"Well, sorry, but you're going to, because this is one of my favourites. I wrote it for my old friend Joel Garner, one of the greatest West Indies fast bowlers. And it was the song that won me my first calypso contest:

If there is one thing that cricket teach me,
Life is a game of glorious uncertainty.
If there is one thing cricket teach me,
Life is a game of glorious uncertainty.

You never know what's around the corner.
Out of the blue life will send down a bouncer.
And just when you think luck ain't coming your way,
Rain will come like a blessing and save the day.

But Count Crawfish say don't leave it all to luck,
There's a time to swing and a time to duck.
You can wheel and deal, you can cheat and lie,
But you can't fool the umpire in the sky.

And behind the stumps I see the Grim Reaper,
Death himself disguised as wicket-keeper.
And when you slip, you slide, and when you nick,
        you gone,
Your score of years numbered before you born.

Today you're on top, tomorrow you fall,
And this goes for politicians and all.

One minute you're in, next minute you're out,
That's what life and cricket is all about.

So next time life send down a bouncer,
Accept it like a cricket philosopher.
Crawfish say don't mind if you poor or you rich,
We all have to face the ups and downs of the pitch.

"Calypsos are about serious things, they about funny things, but they always bursting with life," said the Count. He reached out for Riccardo's song book and opened it. "That is why I like this one."

> Butter-Finger
> catching a ball.
> Butter-Finger
> must make it fall.
> Butter-Finger
> fetching a plate.
> Butter-Finger
> must make it break.

Riccardo couldn't believe his ears. Why had Count Crawfish chosen this of all the hundreds of songs in his book?

"What I like is that it feels real," said the Count.

"As you read it, you see Butter-Finger dropping the ball. Right?"

Riccardo stared at his feet.

"But it's not finished. I wonder why?"

"I didn't write it," said Riccardo, in his quietest voice.

"Who did?"

"Wesley."

"Wesley the *Calypso Club* band singer?"

"Yes."

"Then you finish it for him."

Riccardo was about to reply when the old calypso champion put a hand gently on his shoulder. "One day soon, you sing that song in front of hundreds of people. See if I'm not right, Rikki-Tikki."

Riccardo looked at the Count. This strange old man seemed to know so much, but he never told you what he knew, like teachers do. They had never spoken of cricket before, but the Count had heard all about *Calypso Club* and Wesley and the band. And maybe the dropped catch, too. Who had told him? Uncle Alvin, perhaps? Or was it simply that everyone on the Island knew the story of Butter-Finger?

The conversation puzzled him. He wanted to

forget all about cricket and *Calypso Cricket Club*, but he couldn't stop thinking about the team. It was Martha, of all people, who finally pointed the way for him.

"Guess who I've just seen?" she said that evening.

"Who?"

"Your little wicket-keeper friend."

"Oh?" Riccardo hadn't seen Bashy for days.

"He was very happy."

Riccardo didn't ask why. Getting any story out of Martha was like pulling teeth. She'd tell him eventually, but in her own time.

"They won a cricket match."

"So?"

"So they're playing in the Cup Final."

"What! They beat *Waterloo*?" Riccardo had completely forgotten about the Island Cup. It was unbelievable if *Calypso* had made it to the final.

"I don't know who they were playing," said Martha with a shrug. "The final's on the Oval ground a week Saturday. But I don't suppose you're interested. You don't like cricket now, do you?"

"Who are they playing in the Final?"

"I tell you I don't know. Why don't you go ask Bashy?"

Riccardo's head was in a spin. He couldn't rest till he found out all about the game. Should he ring Natty? Or Josh Duende, the scorer? But when he thought about it properly, there was only one answer. Martha was right – he had to go and see Bashy.

Chapter 9

"You never believe how tense it was," said Bashy. "Waterloo need seven off the last over with three wickets left. Big Lug been bowling rubbish all day – loads of wides – so Natty take him off."

"Bet he was happy," said Riccardo.

"He sulking. He wouldn't speak to Natty after the game. Natty bowls the last over. He keeps the ball right up to the batter so he can't slog and there's no score off the first two balls. Then a lucky edge goes for four and they only need three more. Next ball, and down the pitch goes the batter and misses and I take the bails off. Easy. The next player snicks a single and they need two runs to win off the last ball."

"Just like against *The Saints*," said Riccardo quietly.

"So Natty bowls. It's smacked into the covers. Desmond dives, rolls over and throws the ball in to me. Run out by a metre." Bashy mimed the run-out with a quick flick of his right hand.

"Who scored the runs for us?"

"Natty got 40, Desmond, 35. Me, a duck."

"Bad luck."

"Bad shot. Head in the air and middle stump out of the ground."

"Who we playing in the final?"

"Guess. The big heads of cricket. So-called 'Best Team on the Island'."

"*Windward Wanderers*?"

"Who else? Just because we never beat them before, they think it's a walkover. But they're in for a real big surprise."

"The game's at the Oval?"

"Yeah. Strange thing – it's the first time the Cup Final playing there. It was Count Crawfish's idea. You know, the old Calypso singer. He's the groundsman at the Oval."

"Yes, I know," said Riccardo cagily.

"You coming?"

Riccardo didn't answer.

"Wanderers got a lot of supporters. We need all the fans to come and shout for we." Bashy looked searchingly at his little friend.

"I'll see," said Riccardo.

○ ○ ○

Riccardo said nothing to Count Crawfish about his conversation with Bashy. He was puzzled by a lot of things he'd heard, especially the decision to hold the final at the Oval. The Count didn't mention the game either until the evening before the big day. They were sitting on their bench, surveying the excellent wicket the groundsman had prepared.

"Big game tomorrow, Rikki-Tikki," said Count Crawfish.

Riccardo nodded.

The old man handed Riccardo one of his carefully-guarded samosas and then relented and gave one to the slobbering Jessie, too. "*Windward Wanderers* versus *Calypso*. Everyone says *Wanderers* just have to turn up to win, but I'm not so sure."

"*Calypso* will be champions," said Riccardo firmly.

71

"What makes you say that?"

"Because Natty and Bashy are the best batters on the Island. And Bashy a great keeper, you should see him..."

"I have. I went to the semi-final," said Count Crawfish. "Those *Calypso* boys are cool customers. They play for each other. Team spirit, man."

Riccardo looked at the Count. Why was he taking such a big interest in *Calypso Club*?

"What d'you think of that fast bowler?" asked the Count. "You know, the tall one with the big stick-out ears."

"Leo?" said Riccardo. "He's all mouth."

"But the boy's got speed. If he thinks a bit more, he'll take plenty wickets. You gotta combine speed with brains. And he bowling too short. Pitch it up, man, pitch it up. The captain should talk to him more. It's a lonely job being a bowler, especially when the batsman on top and seeing the ball as big as a breadfruit." One by one, Count Crawfish went through the *Calypso* team, talking about each of the players and how he thought they could improve their game. Riccardo was impressed by his knowledge. The Count knew more about cricket than even Uncle Alvin. Riccardo suspected there was a reason why he was talking to him like this, only he couldn't work out what it was.

"I want you to sit here with me tomorrow," said Count Crawfish.

"Who says I'm coming?"

"That's up to you."

There was a silence, and then the Count smiled. "Did you finish that poem?"

"Which poem?"

"Butter-Finger calypso."

"No."

"I think I've got an ending for you."

"Yeah?"

"Tomorrow. I'll sing it to you tomorrow." Count Crawfish stood up, stretched his legs and shuffled off to finish preparing the wicket for the Cup Final. He waved goodbye from the seat of his old mower as Riccardo and Jessie left the ground.

"Be here at ten," he shouted.

Chapter 10

Next morning Jessie knew they were off to the Oval – she was waiting for Riccardo by the back door. Unfortunately, so too was Martha. Martha wasn't at all interested in cricket, but everyone was going to the ground today and she certainly wasn't going to miss the big occasion. Even their mum said she'd be along later.

It was going to be a very hot day – the heat haze shimmered above the Oval stadium. Flags were flying over the pavilion and there was already a large crowd. Wesley and the *Calypso* band had set up their instruments in the shade of a big mango tree on a grassy mound and they were tuning up.

Count Crawfish was waiting on their bench, though at first sight Riccardo didn't recognise him. The Count wore a smart grey suit and a bright orange shirt and even his beard looked less straggly than usual. Riccardo was forced to introduce Martha to him. Martha could be charming when she wanted and, although she'd never been to the Oval before, she had Count Crawfish chuckling at all her funny cricket questions, like "Do you have to be silly to field at silly mid-on?" and "Why do they call it a maiden over when it's a man bowling?" Fortunately, before it got too embarrassing for Riccardo, she spotted some of her friends in the Ramadhin Stand and left to join them.

"That sister of yours is a born comedian," said Count Crawfish with a broad smile. Riccardo grunted.

Both teams arrived and the players went out to the middle to look at the pitch. Bashy waved to Riccardo and he waved back.

"We should bat if we win the toss. It's a lovely wicket for batting," said Count Crawfish. Riccardo liked the 'we' – he was pleased that the Count was supporting *Calypso*. The old groundsman laid out breakfast on the bench.

There were fried plantains and roti wraps with goat curry and gallons of pineapple drink. He'd even brought along a big goat bone to keep Jessie happy, so that they could eat in peace.

The Count tucked an enormous white handkerchief into the open neck of his shirt and gestured to Riccardo to start eating. Jessie wandered off to the fence by the pavilion with her magnificent prize.

As they ate breakfast, the pretty little ground filled up. Most of the *Windward Wanderers* supporters were grouped together at the far end of the Ramadhin Stand and on the grass at the Pavilion End. The *Calypso* fans gathered on the mound around the band or on the far side of the ground under the palm trees. Riccardo spotted Uncle Alvin in the pavilion talking and gesticulating to his friends. The players made their way back from the pitch to the changing-rooms at the back of the pavilion. Leo took a short cut over the little wicket fence where he was stopped in his tracks by a loud and surprisingly savage growl from Jessie, guarding her bone.

Leo backed up against the fence and froze. "Help!" he cried. "Get that dog off me. Help someone. Help!" Jessie looked up and wagged

her tail and Leo's ears literally quivered with terror. "Help me," he whimpered again.

Bashy, Natty and a few of other *Calypso* players heard the fast bowler's cries and rushed over, expecting to find him being savaged to death by the Hound of the Baskervilles. Seeing only Jessie, they burst out laughing.

"G-get it off me," pleaded Leo. "I hate dogs. Someone take it away." He was almost in tears. Bashy called to Jessie but she was enjoying the new game too much. She growled again, rather playfully this time and gave Leo's hand a big, wet lick. He nearly died of fright.

Riccardo and Count Crawfish had been watching the performance from a distance. "Better go and fetch your dog," said Count Crawfish smiling. "We don't want *Calypso* to lose their big, brave fast bowler."

Riccardo was already on his feet. He grabbed a patty and walked over to Jessie. "Here, Jessie," he said. Jessie didn't need a second invitation. She dropped the bone and bounded towards Riccardo and the patty. Leo shot off like a missile in the other direction.

From a safe distance he shouted at Riccardo, "That your dog, Small-boy?"

"Yes."

"Then get it out of this ground."

"Jessie wouldn't hurt a fly."

"I don't trust no dog. If I have my cricket bat, I give it the Leo treatment."

"You couldn't hit a bus with your cricket bat, big man," said Bashy.

"Time to get changed," said Natty, trying to calm things.

Jessie had finished her patty and the bone returned to her thoughts. Seeing her approaching again, Leo scampered into the changing-room without another word.

● ● ●

The crowd clapped as Natty and Winslow Ventura, the Wanderers' captain, came out to the middle to toss up. Count Crawfish sprang from his seat and beckoned to Riccardo. "We need to start this day properly," he said. "Come on."

He led the way to the mound where the band was still warming up. The Count shook hands with Wesley and, to Riccardo's surprise, took the microphone, made a sign to the band and started to sing:

When they give you a six
And call it a nine.
That ain't cricket, man,
That is politician
Throwing dust in people eye.
And if you fall for the bait,
Then you have a long time to wait
For promises to put bread on your plate.
No, that ain't cricket, man.
Count Crawfish say, fair play is my policy,
I believe in cricket democracy.
That's why the only man getting Crawfish vote
Is the man wearing the umpire coat.

The crowd clapped to the familiar rhythm of the Count's most famous song, and when he finished, cheers rolled round the ground like a Mexican wave. The King of Calypso took a bow and handed back to Wesley, who sang Bat and Ball, with the *Calypso* supporters joining in the chorus. The Count and Riccardo made their way back to their seat with all eyes on them.

On the way they passed Leo's three big-mouth friends, Snapper, K-man and Brian, who nudged each other and sniggered as they saw Riccardo with the old groundsman. An announcement over the loud speaker made Riccardo look up. "The toss has been won by *Windward Wanderers* and they will bat."

"Oi, Small-boy, watch where you put your great clumsy feet!" shouted Snapper. Riccardo looked down and saw that he'd accidentally kicked over a can of drink.

"Sorry," he said.

"Sorry. Forget 'sorry', Small-boy. Go buy me another. There's the drinks tent, see?"

"But it was nearly empty," protested Riccardo.

"I say it was full, Small-boy," said Snapper. "And I got witnesses." K-man and Brian nodded and sniggered.

"So what you waiting for?" said K-man.

"And don't bother spill it, Butter-Finger," said Brian in his squeaky voice, and all three idiots burst out laughing again.

Riccardo didn't move. He didn't like Snapper and his friends. They had a nasty reputation for bullying. Snapper was the most dangerous, always looking for trouble.

"I got no money," said Riccardo, putting his hands in his pockets.

"He got no money," chorused K-man and Brian.

"Then better get some," said Snapper coldly. "Go ask that old goat who singing calypso. He always flush... money no problem."

Count Crawfish had walked away as soon as the argument started and there was no way Riccardo was going to ask him for money. He was about to reply, when his right hand touched something in his pocket. A piece of paper. He took it out and saw it was a dollar note. How on earth had it got there?

Snapper saw the money immediately and pounced. "OK, Butter-Finger, that's mine. I'll get the drink. You'd only spill it."

Still puzzled, Riccardo walked slowly away, ignoring the helpless laughter of Snapper and his mates. There was only one person who could have put that money in his pocket. But why? Was the Calypso King a magician and a mind-reader too?

Chapter 11

Winslow Ventura and Rajab Ali were the two most talked-about young openers on the Island. They were both in the best form of their lives after hitting century opening partnerships in each of their last three games. It wasn't surprising that Wanderers were top of the league and hadn't lost a game all season. *Calypso's* first big task was to dispatch this pair back to the pavilion before they did too much damage.

The *Calypso* band played their team on to the field. Wesley was enjoying himself. He'd turned up the microphone and was singing at the top of his voice. Everyone, except the *Wanderers'* supporters, loved the band and most of the crowd knew all the words of 'Bat and Ball' and sang along with the chorus:

Today Bat and Ball will meet
In a sweet calypso beat.

Then, over by the Ramadhin Stand came the sound of another band – bongos and drums and trumpet.

"Heh, heh, Wesley got some competition," Count Crawfish chuckled. "The *Wanderers*' band warming up."

The girl singer of the band had a sweet but powerful voice. Her first song delighted all the *Wanderers* fans, who couldn't wait to join in:

We are the Wanderers.
We are conquerors.
We done smell victory.
We name on the Island Trophy.
So hang your head in defeat.
Calypso CC you done get beat.

We are the Wanderers.
We are conquerors.
We keep the boundary busy.
We make the runs look easy.
So hang your head in defeat.
Calypso CC you done get beat.

The duel of the rival bands reverberated back and forth across the ground. Riccardo sat back and took out his song book. The words that came rushing into his head described the battle ahead: a struggle, like the surge of the sea.

> Feel how the wind blow,
> Listen how the tide flow.

Both bands fell silent as the game began and Leo ran in and bowled the first ball. It was fired in short and swung down the leg side and the umpire signalled a wide. *Come on, Leo*, thought Riccardo. *Keep the ball low*. And the words in his head took on the rhythm of his song:

> Feel how the wind blow,
> Listen how the tide flow.
> Come on, Leo,
> Come on, Leo,
> Keep the ball low
> Throw the yorker to the batsman toe.

But Leo was all fired up. He kept bowling too short and his first over went for nine runs.

"Natty needs to talk to him," said Count

Crawfish. "That boy needs some friendly advice. If he keeps bowling like this, *Wanderers* will think all their Christmases come in one go."

After two more costly overs, Natty was forced to take Leo off. But now the *Wanderers'* opening pair had got their eye in. After ten overs they had 52 runs on the board and were in complete control.

Wesley and the band tried to rally the fielders, but their heads were beginning to go down. Desmond let a ball go through his legs for four and even Natty fumbled and gave away an extra run. Worse was to come – Leo put down a difficult chance, running in from the boundary. He dived, missed the ball, did a complete somersault and the ball went for four.

Uncle Alvin, on a stroll round the ground, stopped by their bench. He shook hands warmly with his old friend, Count Crawfish, before turning to Riccardo. "Your old team mates are not doing too well," he said.

"We just need a couple of wickets," said Riccardo.

"Can't see where they're coming from," replied Uncle Alvin.

At that moment, the left-hander called for

a quick leg bye and Bashy chased after the ball, did a perfect sliding stop, turned and threw in one movement at the stumps. It was a direct hit, and to Win Ventura's disgust he was given out. Riccardo leapt to his feet and cheered his friend.

"Well done, Rikki-Tikki," said Count Crawfish. "You've got your first wicket. Now how you going to get number two?"

"I'd bring back Leo," said Riccardo.

"But he bowling rubbish," complained Uncle Alvin. "That boy quick, but he got to learn to pitch it up."

"Captain needs to make things happen," said the Count.

"I'd change the bowlers round."

"Slow one end, quick the other – that's the way."

"You're right. Let the batsmen work for their runs."

Riccardo listened to the two old friends talking as he watched the progress of the game. Nothing much changed after the fall of the wicket. The runs continued to flow and it looked as if *Windward Wanderers* were heading for a mountain of a total.

● ● ●

Drinks were taken out for the players with the score at 112 for one. Rajab Ali was on 49. None of the bowlers had beaten the bat all afternoon and the only wicket to fall had been a run-out. *Calypso* were letting the game drift away.

It was then that a crazy thought crossed Riccardo's mind. "Why not?" he said to himself. "Nothing to lose." And, before he knew it, he was running towards the grassy mound.

Snapper and his friends were getting bored with the game and were trying unsuccessfully to start a Mexican wave. They spotted Riccardo.

"Here comes Butter-Finger," said Snapper, "Watch out for them drinks."

"Catch," said K-man, throwing an empty can towards Riccardo. It bounced on to the pitch.

"Pick that up," shouted someone behind them.

The three grinned in dumb insolence and didn't move. Riccardo retrieved the can and placed it in a bin. "Nice one, Butter-Finger!" sneered Snapper.

On the hill the band members were sitting in a heap looking as miserable as the rest of the *Calypso* fan club. They hadn't played a note during the drinks interval, though the *Wanderers'* band had been in full swing. Riccardo walked straight up to Wesley. He talked for a while and

Wesley listened. A smile spread across the band leader's face and he shook hands with Riccardo, who carefully tore a page from his red song book and gave it to Wesley.

The over came to an end and the *Calypso* band started up again:

> Natty, bring back Leo,
> Pace is a blessing,
> Keep the batsman guessing.
>
> Natty, bring back Leo,
> Give the boy another spell,
> Bowl the hurricane in white flannel.

Riccardo watched Natty's reaction to the song as he returned to his seat. He saw the look of surprise on the skipper's face. Then Natty threw the ball to Leo.

The band took up the song again.

> Come on, Leo,
> Come on, Leo,
> Keep the ball low,
> Throw the yorker to the batsman's toe.

Riccardo sat down again between Uncle Alvin and Count Crawfish. "You know, I like that little tune of Wesley's, Rikki-Tikki," said the old calypso singer. "That tune got something."

Chapter 12

Leo's first ball to Rajab Ali was fast and angled into the batsman's boot. The batter just managed to jab down on it in time. The *Wanderers'* opener was still on 49 and looking everywhere for a single, but the big fast bowler kept firing in yorker after yorker and the fielders swooped in and prevented a run being taken. The over ended. The crowd clapped the first maiden of the innings. And the band started up again:

Spin the ball, Natty. Throw the googly.
Spin the ball like Spider Nansi.
Draw the batsman into your web,
Catch him plumb on the leg.
Keep your fingers 'cross the seam of the ball
And Windward Wanderers bound to fall.

Natty gave Wesley a long, hard look and scratched his head. He had been bowling medium-pace seamers from the harbour end. He marked out his run-up again and ran in to bowl. A slow looping delivery turned past the batter's groping bat. Riccardo smiled to himself and crossed his fingers.

"Interesting idea," said Count Crawfish to Uncle Alvin.

"Young Wesley should be captain. He a born leader. And the boy knows his cricket," said Alvin. The Count gave Riccardo a secret wink.

The *Wanderers'* pair took a leg bye and Rajab Ali faced up to Natty. Here was the chance to score the single he needed for his 50. He played a slicing cut at a spinning ball but it wasn't wide enough and the *snick*! was heard all around the ground. Bashy caught the ball and threw it up in the air. The umpire raised his finger.

At the other end Leo kept firing in his yorkers. At last, a direct hit knocked over the middle stump. It was 114 for three and the spring and bounce had returned to the *Calypso* players' steps. Suddenly the fielders were cutting off the singles, diving to stop the boundaries. The crowd realised that they were, at last, watching a contest. A buzz ran round the ground and the rival bands battled it out like the players on the pitch.

As the *Wanderers'* innings reached the final over the score stood at 173 for seven.

"Funny game, cricket," said Uncle Alvin. "I'd have bet my rum shack that *Wanderers* would score 240. Now they're struggling to get past 180."

"Natty's kept up the pressure," said Count Crawfish. "That's the sign of a good captain."

"All thanks to Wesley. That song was the turning-point," said Riccardo's uncle.

Leo bowled the last over. His eyes blazed. Riccardo had never seen him bowl so fast or with such rhythm. When, with his third ball, he held on to a sharp caught and bowled chance down by his boots, Riccardo was on his feet cheering – applauding Leo, of all people. And if the big bowler had taken a hat trick, he'd probably have run out on to the pitch and hugged him. Last ball of the innings, and Leo knocked over the middle stump again. The *Calypso* players walked in with heads high and Leo leading the way. He was clapped and cheered all the way to the pavilion.

The final total was 177 for nine. *Calypso* needed 178 in 40 overs. Not an easy target but, with a good start from Natty and Desmond, they could pull off the surprise of the season.

Count Crawfish and Uncle Alvin went for a cup of tea, leaving Riccardo alone on his bench, where Bashy joined him.

"Did you ever see Big Lug bowl that fast?" asked Bashy.

"He was deadly," agreed Riccardo.

"It was the song that fired him up."

"Wesley's song?"

"Yeah. Except Wesley says he didn't write it. Someone else did."

"Who?"

"He won't say. But I think it was Count Crawfish."

"Why?"

"Because it got that Crawfish touch. No one else can write a calypso like that. We were getting hammered and it gave us back our fight."

Riccardo blushed. "What number you batting?" he asked.

"Five."

"You nervous?"

"Shaking in me pads."

"Don't worry. We bound to win."

Bashy grinned. "At least we winning the battle of the bands." And even as he spoke, everyone on the mound was singing their new favourite again:

> Feel how the wind blow,
> Listen how the tide flow,
> Bat your heart out
> Like there's no tomorrow.
>
> Show them your paddle,
> Your cow-lash, your hook,
> Show them shots from in
> And out of the book.

Chapter 13

Before *Wanderers* took to the field, it rained. The sky went black, the wind shook the palm trees, and for ten minutes it was like standing under a pressure shower. The crowd rushed for the cover of the trees and the overhanging roof of the pavilion. Bright umbrellas appeared. Riccardo sheltered under a sheet of plastic. Then, as fast as the rain had come, it stopped. The sun was out again and the air felt cooler and refreshed.

Count Crawfish returned to the bench with Uncle Alvin. He wiped the water off the seat with an old towel, sat down, looked out at the pitch and frowned. "That'll make batting tricky for a time. The pitch will be bouncier, you'll see."

"We used to call it a sticky wicket," said

Uncle Alvin. "As it start to dry, watch the spinners get the ball to turn and bounce."

"I saw the Island first team get bowled out for 32 on a pitch just like this," said the Count gloomily.

Natty and Desmond made their way to the middle, where the two umpires and the *Windward Wanderers* team were waiting to get the second half of the game under way. The *Wanderers'* opening bowler hurled down a couple of looseners to one of his fielders. The umpire signalled: play. And the first ball fizzed past Natty's helmet as he swayed quickly out of the way.

"See what I mean," said Count Crawfish. "*Calypso* boys are going to need some luck on this track."

"Duck and dive," said Uncle Alvin with a wheezy chuckle.

Natty survived the first over. But then Desmond got a snorter. It struck him a horrible blow on the side of his helmet and he fell to the ground. Natty, the umpires and most of the fielders rushed up to him. Desmond got to his feet unsteadily. He took off his helmet, rubbed the side of his head, put it back on and prepared to face the next ball. It was short and fast. Desmond fended it off with his gloves and the ball spooned up in the air to the keeper. With a shake of the head, Desmond walked sadly back to the pavilion.

Things happened fast after that. The ball was shooting in all directions and the keeper wasn't finding life much easier than the batters. Four byes. Two more byes. A snick through the slips for another boundary. Finally an edge went straight into the keeper's gloves. The next batter was clean bowled... first ball.

Calypso were 13 for three when Bashy joined Natty to face the third ball of a hat trick. He safely fended off another lifter. At the end of the over the band played on, but the disastrous start to the innings had dampened their spirit. And to make matters worse Wesley was losing his voice.

The same couldn't be said for the *Wanderers'* singer. With the fall of each wicket, she sang,

> One more wicket gone!
> Pity the opposition.
> One more wicket gone!
> Trial and tribulation.

Out in the middle Natty and Bashy struggled bravely. The bouncy ball darted about as if it had a mind of its own. They both needed some luck to survive. Natty was dropped in the slips and Bashy edged a ball just past his leg stump. But slowly the scoreboard started moving. It crept up past 20, and 30, and then 40. Riccardo was on the edge of his seat. He knew that one of these two – or both of them – had to make a big score for *Calypso* to stand a chance of winning.

The crowd grew noisier – the *Calypso* supporters cheering every run, the *Wanderers'* fans getting behind the fielders and the bowlers. The *Calypso* band started up again, but as Wesley began to sing, a strange sort of high-pitched wheezing sound came out and his voice finally faded away completely. After a short discussion, one of the players in the band took the microphone and tried his best to sing 'Bat and Ball'.

"This boy sings like a bullfrog," said Count Crawfish, putting his fingers in his ears.

"Stop it, man," begged Uncle Alvin. "It go bring tears to me eyes."

Another band player took over from the first singer but his voice was even worse.

"Lord have mercy, he'll empty the ground," moaned the Count,

The *Wanderers'* fans began to whistle and jeer

at the band and for a time the game of cricket was almost forgotten. Then Natty, possibly unsettled by the singing, hit the ball straight to a fielder and called for a crazy single. Bashy sent him back. Natty slipped, fell, attempted to dive for the crease, but he was well out of his ground when the bails came off. He took one look at Bashy, as if to say, 'It's all your fault', and walked off. And with him went *Calypso's* slim chance of winning the Cup.

The run-out had a strange effect on Bashy. He went mad. He was lucky to survive a wild slog, then he was dropped by the keeper and nearly run out a ball later.

"The boy needs to calm himself," said Count Crawfish.

"They may call him Bashy, but he'll never bash his way out of this pickle," agreed Uncle Alvin.

Another wicket fell, and another. Bashy survived several more close calls. The 50 came up but none of the *Calypso* supporters bothered to clap. Riccardo had seen enough. As he walked towards the band on the hill, he did a quick calculation in his head. *Calypso* needed to score 120 runs in 20 overs. That was six runs an over and they had four wickets left. Ravi had joined Bashy in the middle.

He could bat a bit, but after him came the three bowlers. Mission nearly impossible, he told himself. But not quite.

Wesley saw him approaching and waved. Riccardo was waving back when someone in the crowd stuck out a foot and tripped him up.

"Watch where you're putting your big feet, Small-boy," said Snapper, winking at his friends.

Riccardo picked himself up and stared at Snapper. "You tripped me."

"No way, you fall over your two left feet. That right, K-man?"

Riccardo turned to walk away and Snapper pushed him hard. Riccardo shot out an arm as he was falling and grabbed Snapper's shirt. There was a loud ripping noise.

"You ripped my shirt, you clumsy donkey," shouted Snapper, and the three bullies loomed over Riccardo threateningly.

"Leave him, Snapper," said a barely audible, husky voice. It was Wesley.

"None of your business, Wesley," said Snapper with a scowl.

"I'll decide that," croaked Wesley.

Riccardo picked himself up for a second time. Turning his back on the three bullies he walked nervously up to the microphone. He tripped over a wire and nearly fell again. There was mocking laughter from behind, but he ignored it. He took the mike from its stand but he was so shaky that he fumbled and dropped it.

"Butter-Finger, Butter-Finger," chanted Snapper. His two friends were laughing so much they had to prop each other up.

Riccardo picked up the mike again. The band took up the tune as Riccardo's sweet voice floated across the ground, silencing the crowd in seconds:

> Now is your moment, Ravi and Bashy,
> Now is your chance to make history.
> Don't take your eye off the ball,
> Remember our back against the wall.
> They want you to fall for the bait
> But now is time to consolidate.
> It's up to you, Ravi and Bashy,
> Save the day for Calypso CC.

Chapter 14

The spinner was now bowling and, as Count Crawfish predicted, the ball was turning alarmingly. Nearly every deliver brought a loud appeal from the *Wanderers'* fielders for lbw or a catch close to the wicket. But Bashy battled on. He was determined now – watching the fielders like a hawk and encouraging Ravi, because he knew Ravi usually got out having a wild swish.

"At least we're making them sweat for their victory," wheezed Wesley like an asthmatic frog.

"And who says *Wanderers* will win?" said Riccardo quietly.

"Catch sense, man. After Ravi there's Ryan, Rohan and Leo. And, face it, none of them can bat."

As if to prove Wesley right, Ravi was finally

tempted into one of his swishes, there was a loud *snick*! and the delighted keeper took the catch at the second attempt.

The silenced *Wanderers* band was on its feet again and the singer jubilantly belted out:

> **One more wicket gone!**
> **Pity the opposition.**
> **One more wicket gone!**
> **Trial and tribulation.**

Riccardo watched the *Wanderers'* captain carefully. Would he attack and bring back the fast bowlers now to finish off the innings? No, he played it safe. A new bowler came on at the harbour end, bowling to Rohan, and after one ball Riccardo knew that it was time for *Calypso* to take their chance. In moments he'd written out the words of a new song in his book and he rehearsed it with the band, tapping out the rhythm on a bongo drum.

Riccardo bided his time. He waited for the spinner to finish his last over. Perfect. Bashy was on strike for the new bowler. He stood up and sang:

> Bash de ball, bash de ball, Bashy,
> Show them who's boss of the boundary.
> Don't use your bat like a feather,
> Take the shine off the leather.

Bashy smacked the first ball of the new over into the Low Stand for six and waved his bat towards Riccardo. The second went like a bullet in the opposite direction for four. Another boundary was clubbed straight back past the bowler. Everyone on the mound around Riccardo was on their feet, dancing. The poor bowler wilted under the onslaught and bowled two wides. The fielders were right back on the boundary, but Bashy was hitting the ball so hard that it scorched across the grass. They ran two more runs, then another two to bring up the 100. The final ball of the over was short and Bashy stepped back and pulled it viciously for another four. Amazing... 24 runs had come off the over and the score had leapt to 104 for eight.

Up jumped Riccardo in front of the band again.

> Calypso, you dictate the game,
> Make Windward boys feel the strain.
> Wait for the loose ball to come down
> Then hit it right out the ground.

Winslow Ventura brought back his opening quick bowlers immediately but the big over had shifted the balance of the match. Bashy took as much of the bowling as he could because every time Rohan faced, he looked like getting out. The score climbed slowly in ones and twos. Bashy passed his 50 to tumultuous applause. If he could stay there till the end, there was just a glimmer of hope.

With the score at 131, Rohan finally got a good straight ball and it smashed into the stumps. There was a groan on the mound and a big cheer from the Ramadhin stand. Number 10, Ryan, somehow survived the last two balls of the over.

Everything depended on Bashy now. He decided to try and win the game in fours. But, with most of the fielders out on the boundary, it was no easy task. One four bisected the fielders but mostly they were forced to run risky twos to keep Bashy on strike.

On the mound things were almost as exciting as out on the pitch. Little groups of people were dancing together. Every run got a big cheer, even the wides and no-balls. There were gasps and groans and shouts of advice for the players. Riccardo sang and the band played at the end of every over. Uncle Alvin appeared with Count Crawfish. Martha and her friends turned up, too, and Riccardo's mum was with them. She smiled broadly at him and waved. Behind them, Jessie emerged from the throng wearing a maroon West Indies scarf around her neck. But, Riccardo noticed, there was now no sign of Snapper and his mates.

● ● ●

The match swung back and forth and slowly the score mounted. The 150 milestone came and went. And then, unbelievably, *Calypso* needed 18 more runs to win in three overs.

Ryan was growing in confidence, edging and nudging the ball for singles to get Bashy on strike. The fielders were under pressure. They shouted and screamed at each other as they made more and more mistakes. Bashy hit another four and for the first time *Calypso* were narrow favourites to win.

The last over began with eight needed for victory. Ryan faced up to *Wanderers*' quickest bowler, edged the ball past the keeper and ran.

"Look at foolishness," shouted Count Crawfish. "It's straight to the fielder."

"No!" screamed Bashy. It was too late. Ryan kept running. Bashy hesitated, then put his head down and set off on a hopeless dash down the pitch. The throw came in to the keeper and he gathered it cleanly. There was no need to hurry. With a smile, he flicked off the bails. Bashy was run out by half the length of the pitch.

"I don't believe it," sighed Uncle Alvin, with his head in his hands. "The boy give away his wicket. Why didn't he stand his ground and let the other one get run out?"

Bashy walked slowly back to the pavilion with his head bowed. He knew he'd made the wrong choice in the heat of the moment. He was applauded all the way. He'd scored 88 runs out of a total of 170. But the look on his face said, *I've just lost the game, it's my fault.* The sight of Big Lug emerging from the pavilion and coming nervously out to bat did nothing to make him feel better.

Chapter 15

Leo, it's all in your hands,
Don't disappoint Calypso fans.
Leo, don't blame the sun.
Leo, don't blame the skies.
Leo, for once, open your eyes
Before you look to drive,
Leo, it's all in your hands,
Don't disappoint Calypso fans.

Riccardo's heartfelt song silenced the crowd. Leo waved his bat towards the band as if to say, 'I'll do my best'. He wasn't wearing his shades and Riccardo even thought his ears looked a bit smaller than usual. Without bothering to take a guard, Leo stared down the pitch at the advancing fast bowler. There are nine ways of getting out in cricket and Leo had perfected every one of them. His speciality was clean bowled, middle stump. The bowler reached the end of his run-up. Half the *Calypso* fans closed their eyes. But, for once, Leo didn't. It was a yorker. Amazingly, he jabbed his bat down on it and the ball squirted away.

"Yes!" shouted Ryan, none too convincingly, and they ran a single. There was a sigh of relief as everyone realised Leo wouldn't face the next ball, then a different sort of sigh when Ravi missed completely and the ball whistled past his off stump... so close that the wicket-keeper dropped it in surprise. Leo saw his chance and raced through for a bye.

Now Leo took his time. He even checked the scoreboard. Six runs needed and three more balls.

"Don't slog it yet, Leo," whispered Riccardo under his breath. Everything was now in the big fast bowler's hands. Leo watched the ball and miraculously played a sweet little glance shot but there was only one run in it. Ryan's next delivery was wide down the leg side. The umpire stretched out his arms to signal the extra run and the crowd on the mound cheered as if it had been a six. Somehow Ryan hit the fifth ball into the ground and they dashed through for one more.

So Leo faced up to the last ball of the innings. Three to win. He had to hit a boundary somehow... somewhere. Bashy, still wearing his pads, joined Riccardo on the mound.

"It's over," he said gloomily. "We got close – but Big Lug has never hit a four in his life."

"So this will be his first," said Riccardo, sounding more confident than he felt.

"I can't see where he can hit it. They have fielders all round the boundary."

"Maybe he'll knock a six over their heads. Or he could snick it over the keeper – not a man on the boundary behind him."

The moment of truth had come. The bowler was running in. Leo waited, Lifting his bat up and down. Down came the ball, dead on target. Leo stepped back and swung. There was a loud *snick*! and the ball rose high. At first it looked as if the keeper was going to run back and catch it. But it was just out of his reach and it bounced down towards the sight screen at the harbour end. Two of the *Wanderers'* fielders were after it.

"It's not going to reach the boundary," said Bashy.

"Run, Leo. Run like the wind!" shouted Riccardo. They scampered two runs. The fielder picked up the ball. Ryan turned for the third. He was running to the danger end. The throw was on its way. He put his head down like a charging bull. Ryan was quick – but was he quick enough? The keeper took the ball wide of the stumps just as Ryan dived full length. His bat crossed the line. Off came the bails. "Howzat!" screamed the keeper.

"Not out," said the umpire.

Ryan leapt to his feet, threw his bat in the air and raised his arms high. An enormous cheer enveloped the ground.

Then it was pandemonium everywhere. Bashy and Riccardo were hoisted on to the shoulders of the *Calypso* fans and carried out to the middle of the pitch to greet Leo and Ryan. All around, people were dancing and leaping and singing. Leo and Ryan were also lifted aloft and the four heroes met and swapped high fives. They were carried back to the mound to greet the crowd again. The band started up once more and Riccardo recognised the tune instantly. Count Crawfish was standing at the mike and he sang:

> **Butter-Finger**
> **catching a ball,**

Butter-Finger
must make it fall.
Butter-Finger
fetching a plate.
Butter-Finger
must make it break.
But Butter-Finger
sings so sweetly.
they'd say. 'A pity
he's so clumsy.
Look! The microphone
keeps slipping
and Butter-Finger
keeps tripping.'
Yet a thousand
people applauding
To hell and go
Butter-Finger. the new
Champ of Calypso.

The award ceremony was delayed by the *Calypso* celebrations but the crowd stayed on for the presentations. Even the *Wanderers'* fans clapped loudly when Natty went up to receive the Cup. He raised it high above his head to a huge cheer. Natty went straight over to Riccardo and solemnly handed the Cup to him. Riccardo was so surprised, he nearly dropped it. But he too raised it high in the air. And this time the cheer from the crowd was easily the loudest of the day.

The Man of the Match Award went to Bashy but the judges said that Leo had run him close with his bowling and batting under pressure. And then Count Crawfish stepped forward and said that there was a final award he would like to make on behalf of the judges and *Calypso* CC. One by one, each of the *Calypso* band members was presented with a medal which the Count hung around their necks. Wesley was the last to receive his medal. Not a sound came out of his mouth when he tried to say thank-you into the mike.

"And now, could the reserve singer come up, please," said Count Crawfish. "Rikki-Tikki, the Calypso King."

Riccardo walked hesitantly towards the stage. Of course, he tripped on the first step and everyone laughed as he grabbed the rail to stop himself falling. Count Crawfish took his hand.

As the cheers and whistles died down, Leo appeared on the stage with a beautiful cricket bat and a smile that stretched from big ear to big ear. He presented the bat to Riccardo.

"This is a new bat. *Calypso Club* bought it for today's game," explained Count Crawfish. "It has been used twice – by Bashkar Ali, who scored 88, and by Leo here, who hit the winning runs. So I say it's a lucky bat. And the team wants you to have it, Rikki-Tikki-Tavi."

"Can you bring it to the game next Saturday, Small-boy?" asked Leo.

"Am I playing?" asked Riccardo.

"Of course."

"No he's not. He's singing in the band," wheezed Wesley.

"Time for a song, Rikki-Tikki," said the Count. He put a box against the mike for Riccardo to stand on, and they sang one of their favourite songs together as the crowd clapped happily to the beat:

Listen people, listen all
to this little cricket ball.
Listen people, listen all
to this little cricket ball.
Remember, cricket ball have feelings too.
And in my position you'd be black and blue.
But cricket ball say patience is virtue.

When bat hitting to hell and go,
Is me the ball does feel the blow.
When the crowd calling for six,
Is me the ball does feel the licks.
Yes, is me the ball taking licks everywhere,
When it comes to licks I take my fair share,
But I don't blame bat for this assault
or the bowler for dropping me short.

So rub me, fast bowler, rub me keep me shine,
Bounce me, fast bowler, bounce me down the line,
I the ball biding my time.
Never mind the bat getting the ovation,
I the ball will rise to the occasion.
Soon soon soon I will get my chance
And when ball call the tune, bat will have to dance.
Soon soon soon I will get my chance
And when ball call the tune, bat will have to dance.

Cricket Quiz

Test yourself with this short quiz (answers at the end).

All the words below appear in this book.
Which definition fits the story?

Bouncer
a. Short-pitched ball which reaches the batter at head height
b. Liar and boaster
c. Big man who throws people out of clubs

Googly
a. Person addicted to surfing the internet
b. Surprise ball bowled by a leg spinner that turns in the opposite direction
c. Bird with a long curved bill

Hat trick
a. Magic turn using a chicken and three top hats
b. To take a collection of money
c. Three wickets taken from three consecutive balls by a bowler

Stump

a. Part left when a tree is cut down

b. Wicketkeeper knocks the bails off while the batter is out of the crease

c. Ask someone a difficult question which they can't answer

Maiden

a. Young woman

b. Open space

c. Over in which no runs are scored

Yorker

a. Person from York

b. Ball that bounces under the batter's bat

c. Chocolate bar

MORE GREAT FICTION FROM FRANCES LINCOLN

The Great Tug of War
Beverley Naidoo
Illustrated by Piet Grobler

Mmutla the hare is a mischievous trickster.
And when Tswhene the baboon is vowing to
throw you off a cliff, you need all the tricks you can
think of! Mmutla tricks Tlou the elephant
and Kubu the hippo into having an epic tug of war,
and the whole savanna is soon laughing at their
foolishness. However, small animals should not
make fun of big animals and King Lion sets out
to teach cheeky little Mmutla a lesson...

These tales of Mmutla's tricks, are the
African origins of America's beloved Brer Rabbit
stories. Their warm humour and lovable
characters are guaranteed to enchant
new readers of all ages.

ISBN 10: 1-84507-055-0
ISBN 13: 978-1-84507-055-7

Hey Crazy Riddle!
Trish Cooke
Illustrated by Hannah Shaw

Why does Agouti have no tail?
How did Dog lose his bone?
Why can't Wasp make honey?

Find the answer to these and other
intriguing questions in this collection of
vivid and melodic traditional tales from
the Caribbean. Sing along to these stories as you
discover how Dog sneaks into Bull's party,
why Cockerel is so nice to Weather no matter
whether she rains or shines, and if the dish
really ran away with the spoon!

ISBN: 1-84507-378-9
ISBN 13: 978-1-84507-378-7

Purple Class and the Skelington
Sean Taylor
Illustrated by Helen Bate

Meet Purple Class in these four zany
classroom stories. There is Jamal who sometimes
forgets his reading book, Ivette who is the best
at everything, Yasmin who is sick on
every school trip, Jodie who owns a crazy snake
called Slinkypants, Leon who is great at
rope-swinging, Shea who knows about
blood-sucking slugs and Zina who
discovers something rather disturbing
sitting in the teacher's chair...

Purple class is sure Mr Wellington has died
when they find a skeleton in their classroom.
But is it really Mr Wellington's skelington?
What will they say to the school inspector?

ISBN 10: 1-84507-377-0
ISBN 13: 978-84507-377-0

COMING IN AUGUST 2006

Christophe's Story
Nicki Cornwell
Illustrated by Karin Littlewood

Christophe is a young Rwandan asylum seeker,
now living in the UK with Mama and Papa
and having trouble getting used to
his new school, new language and new life.
Christophe is still learning English so he
struggles with the work that Miss Finch gives
the class. Most of all he misses his grandfather
who they had to leave behind.
When a group of boys discover a scar on
Christophe's chest made by a bullet from the gun
of a Rwandan soldier, Christophe bravely
decides to share his story with his classmates – so
he tells them of the terrifying day
the soldiers came to his house...

ISBN 10: 1-84507-521-8
ISBN 13: 978-1-84507-521-7

Roar, Bull, Roar!
Andrew Fusek Peters and Polly Peters

A year abroad for Czech brother and sister Jan
and Mari means arriving in rural England
in the middle of the night – and not everyone
is welcoming. As they try to settle into their
new school, they are plunged into a series
of mysteries. Who is the batty old lady in the
tattered clothes? Why is their new landlord
such a nasty piece of work? What is the real story
of the ghostly Roaring Bull – and what lies
hidden in the local church? Old legends are revived
as Jan and Mari unearth shady secrets
in a desperate bid to save their family from eviction.
In their quest, they find unlikely allies
and deadly enemies: enemies who will
stop at nothing to keep the past buried.

ISBN 10: 1-84507-520-X
ISBN 13: 978-1-84507-520-0

COMING IN NOVEMBER 2006

Dear Whiskers
Ann Whitehead Nagda
Illustrated by Stephanie Roth

Everyone in Jenny's Class has to write a letter
to someone in another class. Only you have to
pretend you are a mouse! Jenny thinks
the whole thing is really silly... until her pen friend
writes back. There is something mysterious
about Jenny's pen friend. Will Jenny
discover her secret?

"This warm story with a positive message
will make a great choice for newly independent
readers, as a read-aloud, and as
a wonderful introduction to a letter-writing unit."
School Library Journal

ISBN: 1-84507-563-3
ISBN 13: 978-1-84507-563-7